Judy Moody

Around the World in 8½ Days

Books about Judy Moody and Stink by Megan McDonald,
illustrated by Peter H. Reynolds:
Judy Moody
Judy Moody Gets Famous!
Judy Moody Saves the World!
Judy Moody Predicts the Future
Judy Moody, M.D.: The Doctor Is In!
Judy Moody Declares Independence
Stink: The Incredible Shrinking Kid
Stink and the Incredible Super-Galactic Jawbreaker
The Judy Moody Mood Journal
Judy Moody's Double-Rare Way-Not-Boring Book of Fun Stuff to Do

Other Candlewick Press books by Megan McDonald:
Ant and Honey Bee: What a Pair!

Other Candlewick Press books by Peter H. Reynolds:
The Dot
Ish
So Few of Me

Judy Moody
Around the World in 8½ Days

Megan McDonald

illustrated by
Peter H. Reynolds

CANDLEWICK PRESS
CAMBRIDGE, MASSACHUSETTS

First edition 2006

Library of Congress Cataloging-in-Publication Data

McDonald, Megan.
Judy Moody : around the world in 8 1/2 days / Megan McDonald ; illustrated by
Peter H. Reynolds.—1st ed.
p.   cm
Summary: Judy Moody's new friendship with Amy Namey causes problems with
her old friends and the school project they are working on together.
ISBN-13: 978-0-7636-2832-1
ISBN-10: 0-7636-2832-8
[1. Friendship—Fiction. 2. Schools—Fiction.] I. Reynolds, Peter, date. ill.
II. Title. III. Title: Around the world in 8 1/2 days. IV. Title: Around the world
in eight and one-half days.
PZ7.M1487Jg   2006
[Fic]—dc22   2005046908

2 4 6 8 10 9 7 5 3 1

Printed in the United States of America

This book was typeset in Stone Informal.
The illustrations were done in watercolor, tea, and ink.

Candlewick Press
2067 Massachusetts Avenue
Cambridge, Massachusetts 02140

visit us at www.candlewick.com

For the tarantella dancers
of Girl Scout Troop #997
M. M.

To my brothers and sisters,
Andrew, Jane, Paul, and Renee—
all born around the world
P. H. R.

Table of Contents

Rhyme Time 1

Heebie-Jeebies 16

Club Snub 27

Nellie Bly Says Goodbye 37

Bella Tarantella 50

Fratellino Bratellino 64

Addresses and Messes 70

Pickle Chicle 87

No-Talky Rocky vs. Judy Snooty 96

Elf Schmelf 108

Red-White-and-Green Machine 122

Eatsa Pizza 142

Who's

Judy Moody

Way-official card-carrying
member of the
My-Name-Is-a-Poem Club

Dad

One-of-a-kind Dad

Mom

One-and-only Mom

Nellie Bly

Daredevil reporter.
Raced around the world
in 72 days, 6 hours,
11 minutes, 14 seconds

Who

Stink
Stink McFink,
fratellino, bratellino

Frank
Frank the Prank,
a.k.a. Earl the Pearl

Rocky
Rocky No-Talky

Amy Namey
Amy Same-Samey,
gum-chewing girl reporter

Rhyme Time

The girl had a notebook and a clipboard. The girl wore a blue plaid skirt like a school uniform, and not one but TWO watches. The girl had a pencil behind her ear. The girl looked very noticeable in her blue-green glasses.

The girl came over to Judy Moody's lunch table and plopped herself down right beside Judy's friends Rocky and Frank.

She, NOT Judy Moody, looked like she was in a reporter mood.

Who was this important-looking, glasses-wearing girl, anyway? Judy wondered.

"Amy Namey, Girl Reporter," said the girl. "What's the scoop?"

"Um . . . Screamin' Mimi's chocolate mud?" asked Judy.

"Not the ice-cream kind of scoop," said the girl. "The story kind of scoop. I'm a reporter," she said. "Like Nellie Bly, Dare-devil Reporter."

She, Judy Moody, could not believe her ears.

Frank asked, "Is that like Elizabeth Blackwell, First Woman Doctor?"

Judy leaned in closer.

"Check!" said the girl. She wrote something on her clipboard. "I'm from Ms. Valentine's class, 3V. Can I ask you a few questions? For my newspaper?"

"You have your own paper?" asked Frank Pearl.

"Sure!" said the girl. Just then, Super-Important Girl Reporter held out a ketchup-bottle microphone.

"What's your favorite school lunch?" she asked. "Quesadilla pizza, popcorn chicken, or French toast sticks?"

"French toast is *breakfast,*" said Judy.

"Pizza!" screamed Rocky and Frank at the same time.

"Check!" said the girl. She checked the paper on her clipboard.

"I pack my lunch," said Judy.

"How many times a week should the cafeteria have pizza?" she asked.

"Three," said Frank.

"Five!" said Rocky. "Every day! With extra cheese!"

"Check!" said the girl.

Who was this list-checking, clipboard-carrying Pizza Reporter, anyway? And why were Rocky and Frank, Judy's best-ever friends, talking to her?

"You can't really get us pizza every day for lunch," said Judy.

"Why not?" asked the girl. "My mom

knows the lunch ladies. Besides, it's a free country."

"Hey! That's what *you* always say!" Frank said to Judy.

"Do not!"

"Do too!" said Rocky and Frank at the same time.

"Question Number Three," said the girl. "What else would you like to change about Virginia Dare School?"

"Candy machines!" said Frank.

"A swimming pool!" said Rocky.

"A skate park!" said Frank.

"No School Picture Day!" said Rocky. Girl Reporter was writing as fast as they could talk.

"No Pizza Reporters bugging us at lunchtime," said Judy. The girl stopped writing. The girl did not say "Check!"

In spite of herself, Judy got caught up in the moment. "Okay. I have an idea! For real!" said Judy. "Chew gum in school!"

"Yep," said Rocky.

"Yes!" said Frank.

"Check!" said the girl.

"I could work on my ABC gum collection at school," said Judy. "Start one under my desk. Not just at home on the lamp by my bed."

Girl Reporter was writing again.

"*ABC* stands for *Already Been Chewed,*" said Judy.

"I know that," said the girl. "I collect gum too. I've been to the world's best-ever collection of ABC gum. The biggest in the world."

"Huh?" asked Judy.

"Sure!" said the girl. "Bubblegum Alley. It's in California."

"I went to Boston," said Judy.

"I saw it on summer vacation. You walk down this alley between two buildings and there's a Wall of Gum on each side. Chewed-up gum that people stuck there. Some even made pictures and stuff out of gum. I chewed five black gumballs from the machine they have there and added it to the wall."

"No way!" said Rocky.

"Way!" said the girl. "It's like a Gum Hall of Fame. Or a Gum *Wall* of Fame." The girl cracked herself up.

"Double cool!" said Frank.

"I sent away for a Make-Your-Own-Gum Kit," said Judy. Nobody said a word.

"I'd sure like to see a *Wall* of Gum!" said Frank.

"I have a picture of me standing in front of it," said the girl. "It was in my last issue of the paper. See?" She pulled out a page from the back of the clipboard.

WALL OF GUM

"Whoa!" said Rocky. "Weird. Look at all that chewed-up gum!"

"Wow," said Frank. "You really were there!"

"I had my picture in the *real* newspaper once," said Judy.

"Yeah, your *elbow*," said Rocky. Frank and Rocky cracked up.

"Thanks for your ideas," said the girl. "I've got to go talk to Mr. Todd."

"Mr. Todd? That's *our* teacher," said Judy.

"I know. He has a big scoop for me."

"We already know that he's getting married," said Judy.

"She tries to predict the future," Rocky explained.

"And one time she predicted Mr. Todd was getting married. And he is!" Frank announced.

"Wow!" said the girl. "That's a good scoop!" Judy sat up taller.

"Do real reporters wear pencils in their ears?" asked Frank.

"Check!" said the girl. She looked at both of her watches. "Later, alligators!" she called, tucking the pencil behind her ear.

"Wow!" said Frank. "That girl is just like you, Judy!"

"Nah-uh," said Judy.

"Yah-huh!" said Rocky and Frank together.

"You're like twins or something," said Frank.

"Two of a kind," said Rocky.

"Name one thing the same," said Judy.

Judy Moody · Amy Namey

"Amy Namey. Judy Moody. Her name rhymes. Your name rhymes. Same-same!" said Frank.

"So? She has long, not-messy hair and dimples. And she wears glasses," said Judy. "I don't wear glasses."

"She dresses up like Some Lady, First Woman Reporter," said Rocky.

"I only dressed up like Elizabeth Blackwell, First Woman Doctor, once."

"And she collects ABC gum and likes getting her picture in the paper," said Frank.

"And don't forget she gets scoops," said Rocky, "which is like trying to predict the future."

"She probably likes Band-Aids and pizza tables, too," said Frank. "We should ask her."

"And she says weird stuff, like 'check,' all the time," Rocky added.

"I do not say weird stuff all the time," Judy protested.

"It's like they took a machine and made a copy," said Rocky.

"Maybe she's your clone!" said Frank.

"ROAR!" said Judy.

She, Judy Moody, liked being one of a kind. An original. Her mom said she was unique. Her dad said she was an individual. Mr. Todd said she was in a class by herself (even though there were twenty other kids in Class 3T!).

Being unique made Judy feel special. That's the way it is, was, and always would be. *Should* be.

Until now. Until Amy Namey, Gum-Chewing Girl Reporter, moved in.

Now she felt like a NOT-one-of-a-kind, machine-made copy. A two-of-a-kind, un-original, boring old not-stand-alone clone.

Heebie-Jeebies

Judy was helping Stink with his home-
work, quizzing him for a science test.

"Name the four seasons," said Judy.

"Easy. Salt, pepper, ketchup, and mustard," said Stink.

"Seasons of the YEAR, Stink," said Judy.
"Never mind. How about this one. What
makes dew form?"

"When leaves sweat?" asked Stink.

"N-O!" said Judy. "Here's one. You have to know *this*. What is a fibula?"

"Oh, I know. That's like when you tell a lie, but not a really big one. A little one."

"No, Stink. It's a bone! In your leg! Between your knee and your ankle. I think you better study some more. Now, can I ask you a question?"

"I thought that's what you *were* doing."

"Not a science test question. What would you do if you thought there was just one Stink, then you found out there was somebody else out there just like you? Like another Stink?"

"I'd bug you TWICE as much."

"Never mind. I'll ask Mom and Dad."

Judy asked her mom. Mom just hugged her and said, "You're the one and only Judy Moody in my book."

"Is this for science? Or social studies?" asked Dad.

"You don't understand," Judy told her dad. "There's only ONE of you and ONE of Mom and ONE of Stink. But, well, I mean, what if you met somebody and they were just like you? And you didn't feel special anymore?"

"At least I'd have a new best friend," said Dad.

Hmmm. Judy thought about that one. Best friend? Or best enemy?

The next day, Best-Enemy Girl Reporter came up to Judy at recess. "Hi! Remember me?"

"Check," said Judy, frowning.

"You do remember! Your name's Judy.

Right? What's your last name? I want to put your chew-gum-in-school idea in my paper."

Judy perked up. "Moody. Judy Moody."

"Judy Moody? For real? Hey, you rhyme! Just like me!"

"Same-same," said Judy excitedly.

"So, do kids always try to rhyme stuff around you? Like 'Amy Namey, how's Jamie? Want to play a game-y? You're so lame-y.' Stuff like that?"

"I've heard 'Howdy Doody, Judy Moody' and 'Judy Moody has cooties' about ten hundred million times!"

"Exactly! That's so cool we both have the rhyming name thing. You could be in my club."

"I'm already in a club. The Toad Pee Club. With my friends."

"But this is a real club. It's not just for anybody. It's for people all over the world with names that rhyme. It's called the My-Name-Is-a-Poem Club."

"For real?" asked Judy.

"How real is this?" Amy reached into her pocket and pulled out a card. A way-official, real-and-true membership card.

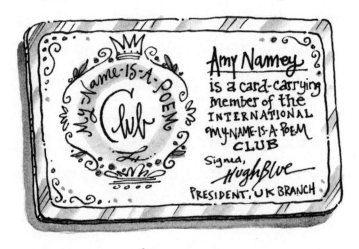

Amy Namey
is a card-carrying member of the INTERNATIONAL MY-NAME-IS-A-POEM CLUB

Signed,
Hugh Blue
PRESIDENT, UK BRANCH

My-Name-Is-A-Poem Club

"RARE!" said Judy. "You mean I could be a member? Of a club that has people in it from all over the whole world?"

"Sure! I can sign you up!"

"You mean I'd get a card like this? A real membership card with my name on it and everything?"

"Check!" said Amy.

"Wow," said Judy. "How come I never knew about you before?"

"Oh, I've been around," said Amy. "Around the world!" She cracked up.

"What stuff do you do in your club?" Judy asked.

"Mostly you just carry this card around. But you can write to anybody in the club.

And sometimes they write back and send you a postcard. With a cool stamp from another country and everything."

"Whoa!"

"I know! I get postcards from people around the world, like, let's see . . . Nancy Clancy, Newton Hooton, and Sing Ling. Even Mark Clark van Ark from Newark! That's in this country. In New Jersey."

"No way!"

"Uh-huh. I even got one from somebody named Heebie Jeebie."

"That gives me the heebie-jeebies."

"I think that one was a joke, for sure. But my favorite is the one I got from Chip Dippe."

"Like potato chips and dip?"

"Exactly." Judy and Amy cracked up.

"I want to do it!" said Judy. "I want to be in the club!"

"Great!" said Amy. "Why don't you come over to my house Saturday morning? I'll get you a membership card and everything."

"I'll ask. Do I have to pay any money?" Judy asked.

"Nope. It's a freebie," said Amy.

"So I won't have to get the heebie-jeebies," said Judy.

"Nopey-dopey!" said Amy.

"Okey-dokey!" said Judy. They fell on the floor laughing.

Amy Namey sure was smart. And funny. And important-looking in her glasses, with two watches, and a pencil behind her ear.

AND her name rhymed. AND she was a member of a way-cool, around-the-world club. AND she knew a top-secret scoop from Mr. Todd.

Amy Namey had all the things that made a New Best Enemy into a New Best Friend.

Club Snub

The next day before going to school, Judy rummaged through her top drawer, looking for her old purple watch. It still worked! She wore it right next to her new red striped one.

She looked around for a clipboard, but she couldn't find one. So she stuck a Grouchy pencil behind her ear and went to school.

"There's a pencil in your hair," said Rocky.

"I know," Judy said. "Amy Namey says I can help her with her newspaper. A good reporter should have a pencil ready at all times."

"How come you're wearing two watches?" asked Frank.

"The better to tell time with," said Judy in a Red-Riding-Hood-and-the-Wolf voice.

"No, really," said Frank.

"Amy Namey has one watch that tells regular time, and one that tells France time. Just like Nellie Bly, Daredevil Reporter. Amy says Nellie Bly always kept one watch on the time it was at home in New York. The other watch she changed to

the time of England or Italy or France—
wherever she was."

"Whatever," said Rocky.

"How come Amy's other watch is on France time?" asked Frank.

"I don't know," said Judy. "I'll just have to get the scoop, won't I?" She took the pencil from her ear and wrote herself a note. Just like a real reporter would do. "Maybe I'll ask her when she comes to our class right after morning recess to tell us a top-secret scoop that only Mr. Todd knows."

"Wait. She's coming here? To Mr. Todd's room?" asked Rocky.

"She's not going to be in our class, is she?" asked Frank.

"No. She just has a big fat secret to tell us."

"How do you know?" Rocky asked.

"I know," said Judy. "Or . . . maybe I can ask her when I *go over to her house* to have a meeting of our *new club.*"

"What new club?" asked Rocky.

"What new club?" asked Frank.

"The My-Name-Is-a-Poem Club," said Judy.

"Can we be in the club?" asked Frank.

"It's for people *all over the world* who have names that rhyme. Like Judy Moody. Amy Namey. Hello! *Frank* does not rhyme with *Pearl*. *Rocky* does not rhyme with *Zang*."

"No fair," said Rocky. "We can't help it that our names don't rhyme."

"I didn't make the rules," said Judy.

"What if I change my name to Earl? *Earl the Pearl* rhymes." Judy and Rocky cracked up.

"Then we'd have to call you Earl," said Rocky. "That would be weird."

"Okay. So keep calling me Frank and come to the Toad Pee Club meeting on Saturday morning. Don't go to that rhyming girl's house."

"What do you mean?" asked Judy.

"Didn't Stink tell you? We're having a really big, important meeting of the Toad Pee Club," said Frank.

"How come?"

"We want to enter Toady in a race they're having at the pet store that morning. Fur & Fangs. You can win a tarantula."

"Stink told you this?" asked Judy.

"Uh-huh."

"It's a girl tarantula named Trudy," added Frank. "It's a painted tarantula and has orange stripes."

"And it has eight eyes, and fangs, and it keeps away robbers," said Rocky.

"Robbers!" said Judy. "There aren't any robbers around here."

"Yah-huh. *Friend* robbers," Rocky said. "Maybe it works on people who steal other people's friends, like Little Miss You-Know-Who."

"Well, sorry, but I have to go to my new club. Amy Namey says—"

"AmyNameyAmyNamey. That girl's all you talk about now," said Rocky.

"Amy Namey sounds lame-y if you ask me," said Frank.

"Ha! Amy Namey *said* you'd say that!" said Judy.

Rocky looked at Frank. Frank looked at Rocky and shrugged.

"What's wrong with you guys?" said Judy. "Yesterday you liked her."

"Yeah, and yesterday you *didn't* like her," said Rocky.

"Just 'cause she rhymes," said Frank. "We were friends with you FIRST. Before Suzy New-Club came along."

"Yeah, along comes Amy Rhymey and you forget about us," Rocky said.

"I bet any money a toad never peed on her," said Frank. "So she can't be in OUR club. No way."

"Shh! Here she comes!" said Judy.

"*Bonjour!*" said Amy Namey. "That means 'hello' in France."

"Whatever," said Rocky.

"Hey, can we ask you a question?" asked Frank.

"Okay, shoot," said Amy. "But hurry up. I have to give a report to your class."

"Did a toad ever pee on you?" asked Rocky.

"What? NO!" said Amy.

"See?" Rocky and Frank said to Judy.

Nellie Bly Says Goodbye

"Class!" said Mr. Todd, blinking the lights. "Morning recess is over. Everybody find your seat. We have a special visitor today. And she has some interesting information to share with us."

"Is it the Crayon Lady?" somebody asked.

"Is *that* the visitor?" asked Bradley, pointing to Amy Namey. "She's just a kid. From Ms. Valentine's class."

"Class, I'd like you to meet Amy Namey," said Mr. Todd. Some kids giggled when he said her name.

Judy practically jumped out of her seat. "I already know her!" said Judy. "And we have three connections. One, her name rhymes, just like Judy Moody. Two, she likes Nellie Bly, Daredevil Reporter, the way I like Elizabeth Blackwell, First Woman Doctor. Three, she collects ABC gum."

"Thank you, Judy. I was about to say that some of you may know Amy from the other third-grade class, 3V, Ms. Valentine's room."

"She lives on my street," Alison S. told Mr. Todd.

"I noticed your colorful glasses before," said Jessica Finch.

"Were you on our field trip to the emergency room?" asked Samantha.

"Why are you always wearing that blue checked skirt?" asked Rocky.

"Why do you have that plastic bread bag full of stuff?" asked Frank.

"Let's give Amy a chance," said Mr. Todd. "She's here to tell us about Nellie Bly, the daredevil reporter who went all the way around the world in seventy-two days."

"Did anybody ever see the movie *Around the World in Eighty Days*?" Amy asked. Only a few hands went up.

"Nellie Bly was a woman reporter," Amy

continued. "She wrote stuff for ne
papers. She read this book about Mr. Fog
He was a made-up person who went
around the world in eighty days. Nellie
thought it would be cool for a real person
to try to beat his record. So her newspaper
sent her around the world. Another
reporter found out and tried to beat her.
But Nellie won the race. She went around
the world in seventy-two days, six hours,
eleven minutes, and fourteen seconds."

Amy Namey looked over at Mr. Todd.

"You're doing great!" said Mr. Todd.

"Someday I want to be a reporter and
travel around the world like Nellie Bly,"
said Amy.

"Why don't you tell us how Nellie

her trip?" said Mr. Todd.

ree days to get ready to

e entire world. And she

e one small bag, the size of a

oread." Amy held up her loaf-of-

ead bag.

"Just think, class," said Mr. Todd. "What if you had to go all the way around the world and you could only take what fits in this bag? What are some of the things you would take? Jessica?"

"A camera."

"Judy?"

"A Grouchy pencil."

"Bradley?"

"Clean underwear." Everybody cracked up.

"Jessica again?"

"My stuffed pig named Snuffles."

"Frank?"

"A hamburger. And my pillow."

"Your pillow's bigger than a loaf of bread," said Bradley.

"Rocky?"

"I'd fill that whole bag with money!"

"Amy, would you like to show us what's in your bag?"

"These are some things Nellie Bly had in *her* bag. Soap. Needle and thread. Pajamas. Slippers."

"No pillow?" asked Frank.

"Underwear," said Amy.

"Told ya!" said Bradley.

"Ink and pens and pencils."

"I called it!" said Judy.

"Three hats, a cup, a raincoat—"

"No way!" everybody exclaimed. Amy unfolded a tiny pouch, and it turned into a raincoat.

"Whoa!" Everybody oohed and aahed.

"And . . . her lucky thumb ring."

Holy macaroni! thought Judy. Lucky thumb ring! A lucky thumb ring was almost as good as a mood ring.

"What about money?" asked Rocky.

"She tied it in a little bag around her neck."

"What about clothes and stuff?" asked Jessica Finch.

"She only wore one dress. It was blue plaid, like this skirt." Amy Namey pointed to the skirt she was wearing.

"What's the stick for?" somebody asked. "Why'd she take a stick?"

"When she got to a country called Yemen, she had to brush her teeth with a stick."

"I can't believe there's a country called Yeah Man!" said Frank.

"And she saw camels and people riding elephants, and when she was halfway around the world, she got a pet monkey named McGinty!"

"Amy, why don't you show us Nellie Bly's around-the-world route on your globe?" said Mr. Todd.

"Okay. I made a globe this morning. It's still kind of wet." She held up a big gloppy papier-mâché ball. "Here's where she started, in Hoboken."

"She started in Hobo Land?"

"Hoboken is in New Jersey," said Amy. "And she went to England, France, Italy. Then Egypt, in Africa." The route was marked in black marker. Amy traced it with her finger.

"Can somebody help me hold this?" asked Amy.

"I will!" said Frank.

"Me too," said Rocky.

Judy could not believe her ears. Ten minutes ago, Rocky and Frank were calling Amy a robber. A big fat friend-stealer.

Now they were helping her!

Frank held the papier-mâché globe. "Where's that Yeah Man place?" he asked.

"I see it," said Rocky. He went over to the bulletin board and pulled out a thumbtack. "It's right down here, on the Red Sea." As he said it, he stuck the pin into the globe to mark the spot.

POW! A loud pop made everybody jump. Frank leaped backward. It was the balloon inside the papier-mâché globe! All the air went out of the globe with a *whoosh,* and it collapsed in on itself.

Frank looked at Rocky. Rocky looked at Frank. "Globe explode!" Rocky said, cracking up.

Amy Namey stood in front of the whole entire Class 3T, holding a mushy, gushy mess of wet newspaper. A slobby-blobby, ooey-gluey globe of gloop.

"Nellie Bly says goodbye!" said Amy, and she rushed out of the room.

Bella Tarantella

Judy passed a note to Frank, who passed it to Rocky.

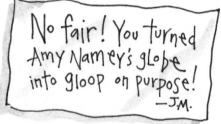

Rocky passed a note to Frank, who passed it to Judy.

Judy was about to pass another note when Mr. Todd told the class it was time for the big scoop. She sat up straight as a pencil.

Mr. Todd was drawing a map on the board. Judy hoped a map was not the big surprise.

"Class, we're about to start a whole new way to learn geography," Mr. Todd announced. "Class 3T is going to go around the world in eight days!"

"What? Huh?" everybody asked.

"We're going to work with Ms. Valentine's class—"

"Yippee!" said Judy. "That's Amy Namey's class." Rocky and Frank frowned at her.

"We'll make a big map like the one on the board and put it up in the hallway between our classrooms. Then we'll trace the journey of First Around-the-World Woman Reporter Nellie Bly. We'll learn about all the countries she visited."

"Did she go to Italy?" asked Rocky. "My grandma's from there."

"Yes," said Mr. Todd.

"Did she go to Disneyland?" asked Bradley.

Mr. Todd chuckled. "I'm afraid not." He wrote the names of eleven countries on the board.

"We'll get into small groups, and each group will take a country. Here are some

things you might try to find out about for each country."

Mr. Todd pointed to the board:

A) WHAT THE FLAG LOOKS LIKE
B) TRADITIONAL FOOD FOR YOUR COUNTRY
C) HOW TO SAY HELLO AND GOODBYE
   OR COUNT TO TEN IN YOUR
   COUNTRY'S LANGUAGE
D) ANY GAMES THAT STARTED IN
   YOUR COUNTRY

"We have only eight days to get all the way around the world, so we're going to have to work fast. There's a lot to learn, a lot to do."

"Can we bring in something real from that country?" asked Jessica Finch. "I have a nesting doll from Russia."

"I'm sorry. That's not one of the countries we're studying," said Mr. Todd.

"I have money from Italy," said Rocky. "And some *carbone dolce*. It's black rock candy that looks like coal."

"Ooh, I have tea from London," said Judy. "That's in England. And I have a cuckoo clock in my bedroom that my grandma Lou brought me all the way from Germany."

"Tell you what," said Mr. Todd. "These are all good ideas, but let's wait until you know what country you'll be working on."

"Is this the big scoop?" asked Frank. "Geography?"

"Yes," said Mr. Todd. "I'm afraid it is. But I haven't told you the best part. We are going to kick off our Around-the-World tour with . . . a movie."

"Movie! What movie?" somebody asked.

"You mean we get to watch a movie in school?" asked Frank.

"Do we get to turn out the lights and have popcorn?" asked Jessica Finch.

"We'll see," said Mr. Todd. "The movie is *Around the World in Eighty Days!*"

"Yippee!" everybody yelled.

That afternoon, the whole class got to go to Ms. Valentine's room and watch the movie. Judy sat on the floor next to Amy Namey. They ate blue popcorn (made from blue corn!) and laughed at this inventor guy named Mr. Fogg, who was trying to fly and flew right through a painting! And he was trying to race around the world in eighty days and some old guys kept calling him a nincompoop!

After the movie, Judy went back to class and got into her small group with Rocky and Frank and Jessica Finch. They chose Italy for their project. They went to the library to look up some books on Italy.

"What's red, white, and green all over?" asked Rocky.

"A Christmas elf?" asked Jessica.

"A pizza with green peppers?" asked Frank.

"No! The flag of Italy," said Rocky.

"Hey, that's funny!" said Judy. "We could start off with a joke like that."

"We could dress up in red, white, and green," said Jessica.

"Yeah!" said Judy. "I love dressing up crazy!"

"Okay," said Rocky and Frank.

"Let's definitely have pizza," said Rocky.

"Yeah, pizza!" said Frank.

"Let's think of something different," said Judy. "Everybody already knows about pizza."

"So? Pizza's the best!" said Rocky. "Italy without the pizza is like Judy without the Moody!"

"How about a pizza spelling test?" asked Jessica Finch. "We could spell words that are on pizza, like P-E-P-P-E-R-O-N-I."

"Not you, too," said Judy.

"We could spell other stuff besides just pizza words," said Jessica. "Like *spaghetti, parmesan,* and *P-I-N-O-C-C-H-I-O.*"

"Not even grownups can spell the word *Pinocchio,*" said Rocky. "Everybody would flunk."

"We could make a Leaning Tower of Pizza!" said Frank.

"Out of what?" asked Judy.

"Pizza tables! You collect them," said Frank.

"Yeah, we could glue them all together into a tower," said Rocky.

"No way!" said Judy. "I'm not letting you go all glue-crazy on my whole collection. Stick to eating paste."

"Nobody's eating paste," said Rocky. "Just pizza."

"You guys have pizza on the brain," said Judy.

"Then let's hear your un-pizza brainy ideas," said Rocky.

Judy pointed to a picture in the book of people dancing in a circle. "We could do this. Dance the tar-an-tell-a."

"I don't know how to dance," said Rocky.

"Especially the tarantula," said Frank.

Mr. Todd passed by their table and saw the picture. "A dance from Italy is a very good idea," said Mr. Todd. "*Bella Taran-tella.*"

"See?" Judy grinned. "It's a very good idea."

"It'll take some practice," said Mr. Todd. "But you'll get the hang of it."

"My grandma has an old record of that dance," said Rocky.

"Let's all go to Rocky's to practice," said Judy. "How about Saturday?"

"Can't!" said Rocky. "Frank and I will be at Fur & Fangs. Not like *some* people." He gave Judy the hairy eyeball.

"I meant Saturday *afternoon,*" said Judy. "I'll be back from Amy Namey's by then."

"I'd love to go to Rocky's on Saturday," said Jessica. "Sounds fun."

"I don't know," said Frank. "The only time I tried to dance was around the May-pole in first grade. I tripped and got all tangled up in streamers and ended up looking like a human candy cane."

"No human candy canes. We promise," said Judy.

"Okay, then, everybody. How about we meet at my house on Saturday at two o'clock?" Rocky said.

"C'mon, it'll be fun!" Judy elbowed Frank.

"Yeah, maybe if you're an eight-legged spider," said Frank.

Fratellino Bratellino

On Saturday morning, Dad agreed to take Judy to Amy Namey's house. Judy checked to make sure she had on BOTH of her watches. Her purple watch was set to regular time in Virginia. Her red striped watch was set to Italy time. And she wore her mood ring on her thumb so she could have a lucky thumb ring just like Nellie Bly, Daredevil Reporter. "*Ciao*, Mamma! *Ciao*, Stink!"

"Why do you keep saying *chow*?" asked
Stink. "Like it's time to eat or something."

"Or something! Don't have a cow, Stink.
It's Italian," said Judy. "I'm learning words
from Italy for our Around-the-World-in-
Eight-Days project at school."

"You mean your Drive-Your-Family-

Crazy-in-Eight-Days project, don't you?" asked Stink. Mom and Dad laughed.

"N-O!" said Judy.

"Does *chow* mean 'hello' or 'goodbye'?" asked Stink.

"BOTH!" said Judy.

"Weird," said Stink. "'Hello' means 'goodbye' in Italy? What a country!"

"*Ciao, bambino,*" Judy said to Stink.

"*Bambino?* Isn't that a baby?" asked Stink. "I am not a baby!"

"Okay, then, *ciao, fratellino.*"

"What's that?"

"'Little brother.' Wait, no. I'm wrong. Oh, yeah, I remember now. It's *BRATellino!*"

"Is not."

"Ya-huh! I mean, *sì,*" said Judy.

"How come you have on two watches?" asked Stink.

"You know how two heads are better than one?"

"Yeah. And two cuckoo clocks make you twice as cuckoo?"

"No," said Judy. "Two watches are better than one, too."

"Oh," said Stink. "Where are you going, anyway?"

"To Amy Namey's house."

"But what about the Toad Pee Club? This morning we race Toady at Fur & Fangs. I might win a tarantula."

"*Buona fortuna,*" Judy said.

"What's tuna fish got to do with anything?" asked Stink.

"Nothing. It means 'good luck,'" said Judy. "I don't know how to say 'bug off' in Italian."

"But you're the one who always says Toady belongs to the whole Toad Pee Club, not just me. So we should all go. Together. That's what makes it a *club*."

"Stink, don't you get it? I'm in a new club now. And today I'm going to get my own way-official, real-and-true membership card. For sure and absolute positive."

"What club? Can I be in it? I want a way-official membership card."

"It's the My-Name-Is-a-Poem Club, Stink. Sorry. It's only for people who have a name that rhymes. So unless you changed your name to Stink McFink—"

"I don't care. I'll be Stink McFink," said Stink.

"No way, Stink McNay. No dice, Stink McLice. No go, *bratellino.*" Judy cracked herself up all the way to the car.

Addresses and Messes

"Ciao!" Judy said to Amy.

"Bonjour!" Amy said to Judy. Amy's group was doing France for their Around-the-World-in-Eight-Days project. "I like your lucky thumb ring! I have one too." She held out her hand.

"Same-same!" said Judy.

"Want to see my ABC gum collection?" Amy asked.

"Check!" said Judy.

"C'mon upstairs." Amy opened a funny-shaped door at the back of her room. It went to a small room under the stairs. "You have to duck or you'll bump your head," said Amy.

"Who lives here? Elves?" asked Judy.

"It's my secret place," said Amy. She pointed to the wall. Chewed-up gum was stuck all over the wall behind the staircase, where nobody could see.

"WHOA!" said Judy. "You started your own Wall of Gum! Just like the one in California."

"Shh!" said Amy. "I don't want my mom to find out."

Judy pretended to zip her lips. "Zipper Lips!" said Amy, and they cracked up.

"Lipper Zipper!" said Judy, and they cracked up some more.

"Want your membership card?" asked Amy. "I sent away for it."

Amy handed the card to Judy. It looked way official. And it was signed by Hugh Blue, just like Amy's.

"Rare!" said Judy. "How did you get yours covered in plastic like that?"

"Tape!" said Amy. They taped up Judy's card to make it look even more official.

"It also comes with this stuff," said Amy.

Judy took the stuff out of the bag. There was a HI, MY NAME IS nametag, a My-Name-Is-a-Poem Club bike decal, a list of members with rhyming names from all

over the world, and a game called the
Name Game.

Judy and Amy played the Name Game.
Judy made up rhyming names for Rocky,
Frank, and Jessica Finch. She made up
eight names for Stink.

Stink McFink   Stinky Pinky
Stink LeWink   Stinky Blinky
Stinky Dinky   Stink the Shrink
Stink's a Jinx   Stink-a-Link

"Stink McFink is still the best," said Judy,
laughing.

"Hey, I know," said Amy. "Let's write to
some real people who rhyme."

"RARE!" said Judy. She took out her list.

"Just think," she said. "Now my name will be on the list someday. Judy Moody."

Amy got out a big plastic tub with all kinds of writing paper and smelly markers, colored pencils, stickers, rubber stamps, and glitter-glue pens.

"Blue glue!" said Judy.

"We can make our own postcards," said Amy. "I can print some out on the computer, even. Then we can send them to other people in the club."

"Okay," said Judy. "I'll send one to Larry Derry Berry, Viola Gazola, Yankee Pankee, and Herman Sherman Berman. Can you believe there's a person in the club named T. Hee? No lie."

"T. Hee. That's funny," said Amy.

"Tee-hee-hee!" shouted Judy and Amy. They both cracked up.

Amy looked at the list. "I'll write to Lance France, Roos Van Goos, Pinky Dinky, and Wong Fong from Hong Kong."

"You made that up," said Judy.

"Nope. It says so right here!" Judy and Amy fell on the floor, laughing some more.

Judy and Amy made postcards all morning. Judy wrote addresses on all her postcards till her hand almost fell off. "Done!" she said.

"I'm not done yet," said Amy. "Why don't you do one more?"

"Okay," said Judy. "How about Nathaniel Daniel? He's from the United States. San Luis Obispo, California."

"Let me see that!" said Amy. She looked at the list. "That's where Bubblegum Alley is. The real Wall of Gum. No lie."

"No way!" said Judy. "Let's send him some gum and see if he'll stick it on the wall for me. Then we can BOTH be on the Wall of Gum."

"Okey-dokey!" said Amy.

"Let's break out the Make-Your-Own-Gum Kit I sent away for," said Judy. "I'm so glad I brought it. I've been dying to try it out. Now we can make our own gum to send him. Will it be okay with your mom?"

"Sure," said Amy. "As long as we clean up."

Judy and Amy went downstairs to the kitchen. "Let's have some lunch first," said Amy. "Mom left us baloney and cheese sandwiches, but I like to cut them up, like this." She took out some cookie cutters, and the girls made sandwiches into stars, hearts, footballs, pumpkins, and rabbits. Judy even made one of the United States (except where Florida broke off).

Amy took the plate over to the table. "We'll never eat all these in a million years," said Judy.

"They're way more fun to make than eat," said Amy, grinning at Judy with a milk mustache.

After lunch, Judy looked at her red watch. She looked at her purple watch. Which was which again? Wearing two watches sure could get a person all mixed-up. But it was still early on BOTH watches.

"Do you have to go?" asked Amy.

"Nope. I have loads of time before I have to go to Rocky's to practice the tarantella dance," said Judy. "Let's turn this puppy loose!" She opened up the Make-

Your-Own-Gum box and held up a bag. "This must be the gum base. It's called chicle. It comes from the rain forest."

They poured bags of powder stuff and sticky stuff into a bowl. They melted it in the microwave.

"I need the mixing tool," said Judy.

They took turns mixing and stirring, mixing and stirring. Powder stuff flew in the air and everywhere. Sticky stuff stuck to the spoon and the chair and the table.

"Now for the fun part!" said Judy. They plopped a big sticky blob down onto some wax paper.

"It says to knead it like bread," said Amy.

"Dive in!" said Judy. They each took a big blob.

"Wait! We better take off all our watches," said Amy. "It's so sticky!"

"Icky, yicky, sticky!" said Judy.

"Ooey, gooey, chewy," said Amy.

Judy pushed back her hair. Judy scratched her nose. Judy dropped some on her knee.

"You have gum all over you!" said Amy.

"So do you," said Judy. "Double bubble trouble!" They cracked up.

"Now for the best part," said Judy. "Flavors. They only give you two. Peppermint and Tutti-Frutti."

"We can make our own," said Amy.

"Like what?"

Amy looked in the cupboard. "Peanut-butter gum? Tuna-fish gum?"

"I don't think so!" said Judy.

Amy looked in the spice rack. "How about cinnamon gum? Vanilla gum? Rainbow-sprinkle gum?"

"Sure!" said Judy. "Why not?"

Amy looked in the refrigerator. "Ketchup gum? Mustard gum? Pickle gum?"

"That's it!" said Judy.

"Ketchup gum? Yick!"

"No!" said Judy. "Pickle gum." She poured some pickle juice from the jar and kneaded it into one of the blobs. "I can take some home to play a trick on Stink.

He'll never know. I'll call it Pickle Chicle."

"A Pickle Chicle trick?" asked Amy.

"Exactly!" said Judy. "A Pickle Chicle trickle!"

They rolled and pressed and squeezed and stretched the gum until it was flat. Then they dusted it with powdered sugar and cut it into pieces.

"Let's taste some," said Judy.

"Not the pickle gum, though," said Amy.

Judy popped one, two, three pieces of gum in her mouth. The gum stuck to her teeth. The gum stuck to her tongue. The gum stuck to the roof of her mouth.

"Is so sicky," said Judy.

"Sicky?" asked Amy.

"Stick-y!" said Judy. "My mouth feels like a hippo eating a jar of peanut butter!"

Amy popped one, two, three pieces in her mouth. Judy Moody and Amy Namey chewed and cracked and blew and popped gum until Judy's dad came and it was time to go.

She, Judy Moody, chewed her Peppermint Rainbow-Sprinkle Tutti-Frutti NOT Pickle Chicle gum all the way home.

Pickle Chicle

"*Ciao!* I'm home!" called Judy as she walked in the door. Stink came pounding downstairs. When he saw Judy, his mouth dropped open.

"Stink? Are you trying to catch flies?" said Judy. "Your mouth's way open."

He laughed and pointed. There was gum in her hair, gum on her nose, gum on her pants, gum on her coat.

"What happened to you?" asked Stink. "Attack of the Killer Gumball?"

"Hardee-har-har, Stink. I was making gum at Amy Namey's with my Make-Your-Own-Gum Kit. It was way fun."

"Aw, you didn't wait for me?"

"No, but I made some special just for you. My own secret recipe." Judy opened up the wax paper and held out the gum for Stink to see.

He saw pink gum, brown gum, gray gum, green gum. And gum with lumps. "Eeuww! I'm not eating that lumpy, bumpy gum!"

"Yours is the green one," said Judy.

Stink picked up the green gum like he was picking up a worm.

"Just try it!" said Judy. "You'll like it!"
She blew a bubble and popped her own
gum.

Stink put the gum in his mouth. He
rolled it around on his tongue. He chewed
it. Once, twice.

"BLUCK!" said Stink, sticking out his tongue. "It's really sour. Worse than sourballs. What is this, anyway? Salt gum?"

"It's Pickle Chicle!" said Judy. "Get it? Pickle-flavored gum! I made it with pickle juice!"

"BLAH!" went Stink, spitting the gum across the room. Mouse pounced on it.

"Gross!" said Judy.

"Stink," said Dad, "pick that up and put it in the garbage can."

"Isn't Judy even in trouble? She tricked me with pickle gum!" said Stink.

"I think you'll live," said Dad.

"It probably had spider eggs in it!"

"Spider eggs?"

"That's my fault," said Dad. "I was

telling Stink how when we were kids, there were all these rumors that gum had spider eggs in it," said Dad. "We were actually afraid to chew gum."

"Weird!" said Judy.

"Speaking of spiders, guess what I got at Fur & Fangs!" said Stink.

"You mean Toady won the race?" asked Judy.

"Not exactly," said Stink. He held out a sandwich bag with a gross-looking spider skin in it. "It's a molted spider."

"A melted spider?" asked Judy. "Gross!"

"Mol-ted. It's just the skin. Spiders have their skeleton on the outside, and they shed."

"Rare," said Judy, peering into the bag.

"Toady wouldn't even hop once when it was time for the race. So the kid who won the tarantula gave it to me. I think he felt sorry for me."

"Tarantula!" cried Judy. "Holy macaroni! I was so busy at Amy's house, getting the scoop on the My-Name-Is-a-Poem Club and tricking Stink with pickle gum, that I forgot I was supposed to go to Rocky's! To practice the tarantula. I mean, the tarantella. Now *I'm* saying it."

"Here's a scoop for you," said Stink.

"Your friends aren't talking to you. I was supposed to tell you. Rocky called. And Frank called. Then Rocky called again. And that Jessica Finch person."

"Stink! Why didn't you tell me? What did they say?"

"They said to tell you that they're really mad you didn't show up and they are not doing the spider dance with you even if you pay them one million dollars."

"Judy, this sounds like a real mix-up," said Mom. "You were supposed to be working on a school project with Rocky and your other friends, but you were with Amy?"

"I didn't do it on purpose, Mom, and now they're mad and they'll never talk to me again."

"It'll work out, honey. Everybody makes mistakes," said Mom.

"We know you're excited about your new friend, Amy," said Dad. "All we're saying is you need to take care not to forget about your old friends, too."

"I can't help it if they're mad," said Judy. "What do I say?"

"Just be honest," said Mom. "Tell them you lost track of time."

"Or tell them the Pickle Gum Monster took over your brain," said Stink.

"Yipes stripes!" Judy said. "I just can't believe this happened. I was getting all mixed up wearing two watches. Then I took off BOTH watches to wash my hands at Amy Namey's. . . . I must have looked at the wrong one or something."

"So I guess you could say TWO watches AREN'T better than one!" said Stink.

No-Talky Rocky vs. Judy Snooty

Judy called Rocky. "I'm sorry I'm late, but my two watches got me all mixed up and then I got attacked by a giant gumball and—"

"I'm not talking to you," said Rocky.

"You just did!" said Judy. "So you're NOT not talking to me!" She laughed. But Rocky did not crack up one teensy bit.

"I mean it," he told her. "Frank's mad, too. He already went home. And Jessica

Finch doesn't even want to be in the group. She's making up her own Pizza Spelling Test."

"But we have to practice the dance! I'm coming over right now."

"Don't!" said Rocky. "I told you—I'm not talking to you."

"But I—we have to. You can't just—"

"*Hmm-hmm, hmm-hmm, hmm hmm hmm . . .*" Rocky would not listen. He just hummed "Twinkle, Twinkle, Little Star" into the phone.

Judy hung up the phone and went to find Stink. "You gotta come over to Rocky's with me," she said. "Now!"

"How come?"

"Because he's not talking to me."

"So?"

"So, he's NOT not talking to you."

⊚   ⊚   ⊚

Judy ran across the street and rang the bell. She made Stink stand in front of her. Rocky opened the door.

ROCKY: Stink, tell Judy I said I'm not talking to her.

JUDY: Stink, please tell Rocky that we have to practice our dance.

STINK: Judy says you have to practice your dance.

ROCKY: Tell Judy that *she's* the one who didn't show up to practice. I don't want to dance like a spider anyway. I quit.

STINK: He quits.

JUDY: I heard. Please tell Rocky I had a really good excuse. Tell him about Attack of the Giant Gumball and everything.

STINK: She did get gum all over her. See? Look at her gum-wad hair.

ROCKY: Tell Judy too bad. It's too late. We waited till after three o'clock and Frank and Jessica Finch went home. And tell her we Q-U-I-T quit.

STINK: He Q-U-I-T quits.

JUDY: Stink, please tell Rocky he can't quit because if we don't do our project, we won't make it around the world in eight days.

Does he want to ruin it for everybody? For Class 3V too? Does he want us to F-L-U-N-K?

STINK: Do you want to flunk and ruin it for everybody?

ROCKY: You already ruined it. I mean, tell Judy *she* already ruined it. If we flunk, it will be all her fault.

STINK: Rocky says—

JUDY: Tell him I'm super, super sorry. I got all mixed up with my two watches 'cause one was on Italy time, but I'm here now, aren't I?

ROCKY: Tell Judy it's not just about for- getting the practice today.

She quit us, her best friends, for
Amy Rhymey. Tell her we can
rhyme too.

Rocky handed a piece of notebook
paper to Stink.

ROCKY: Here, read this.

JUDY: Read it, Stink. Let's hear it.

STINK: I think you should pay me a
quarter if I have to read stuff, too.

JUDY: Just read it!

STINK: *My name is Frank.*

You can call me Frank the Tank.

When Judy didn't show up for practice,

It really stank.

ROCKY: Not that one. This one.

STINK: *My name is Rocky.*

I like hockey.

Really it's the only thing

That rhymes with Rocky.

I don't feel too talky.

Don't mean to be rudey—

I'm just mad at my friend

Judy Snooty.

STINK: Judy Snooty! That's a good one.

JUDY: Hardee-har-har.

STINK: Wait! There's one more:

My name is Stink.

I'm not a fink,

If that's what you think.

I just want a quarter—

JUDY: Stink! You just made that up.

ROCKY: Tell her Frank and I are quitting her.

JUDY: Fine.

ROCKY: Fine.

STINK: Judy's not doing the dance all by herself!

JUDY: Stink, tell Rocky I did not say that. I'll do the dance myself.

STINK: You can't! How are you going to do a spider dance yourself? A spider

has eight legs! You need four
people.

JUDY: Stink! Just tell him.

STINK: She'll do the dance herself.

ROCKY: Stink, ask her why doesn't she just
get her New Best Friend, Amy
Same-Samey, to do the dance with
her?

STINK: Ha! That's a good one! Judy, did
you hear—

JUDY: Ha, ha—so funny I forgot to
laugh. Stink, please tell Rocky I
can't do the dance myself
because he has the old record
of the tarantella from his
grandma. And tell him he has
the old record player, too.

ROCKY: Ha! So now you want to be friends
again, huh? Because you need
something.

STINK: Rocky says—

JUDY: Stink, ask Rocky, Will he at least
bring the stuff to school?

ROCKY: Um . . .

STINK: He said *um*.

JUDY: Um, he'll bring it? Or, Um, he's
thinking about it?

STINK: Rocky, what does *um* mean?

ROCKY: Um thinking! Get it?

STINK: I think he's thinking.

JUDY: Tell him I'm looking at BOTH
my watches, and he has ten
seconds. Nine, eight, seven—

ROCKY: Tell her I'll bring the record and

record player, but I won't do the
dance.

JUDY: Fine.

STINK: She said *fine*.

ROCKY: Fine.

STINK: He said *fine*.

JUDY: Fine.

STINK: I can't believe I'm not getting
paid for this!

Elf Schmelf

On Monday, when Judy got to school, she went to talk to Mr. Todd first thing.

"Mr. Todd," said Judy, "you know how we're going around the world in eight days?"

"Yes," said Mr. Todd.

"And you know how my group is supposed to do Italy?"

"Is there a problem?" asked Mr. Todd.

"Kind of. I mean, yes. We can't do Italy. Or any country."

"I'm sorry to hear that," said Mr. Todd. "Because not just our class, but Class 3V, too, is counting on going around the world in eight days. And we can't go around the world without Italy."

"It's sort of my fault," said Judy. "I missed a practice for the tarantella and Rocky and Frank and Jessica got mad and—"

"I'd like you to try to work this out yourselves," said Mr. Todd. "Just do your best, okay?"

"I'll try," said Judy. "Jessica came up with something she'll do herself, but I know Rocky and Frank, and they can stay mad way longer than eight days."

"Well," said Mr. Todd, "tell you what. How about if we visit Italy last? We can wait till Day Eight and do it at the very end."

"Thank you," said Judy. "Thank you, Mr. Todd. I'll figure it out. Or something."

❧ ❧ ❧

All week, Class 3T, along with Class 3V, had a blast going around the world. Judy tried to forget all about Rocky and Frank being mad at her. In London, Judy and Amy got to say "Brilliant!" And they got to eat chips (a.k.a. French fries) with vinegar.

In France, Amy Namey led the two

classes in singing *"Frère Jacques"* in a round.

In Yeah Man (a.k.a. Yemen), they got to eat spicy beans and rice with their fingers! Then they got to try brushing their teeth with a stick, like Nellie Bly!

In Egypt, they built a giant sugar-cube pyramid. And in Japan, Judy got to try on a kimono and learn kirigami, the Japanese art of paper cutting. In China, they made brush paintings and ate fortune cookies (that were really from the Happy Garden Chinese Restaurant, not China!).

"What does your fortune say?" Judy asked Amy Namey.

You will find new friends soon.

"Nice!" said Judy.

"How about yours?" asked Amy. "What's it say?"

"Nothing," said Judy.

"It's blank? It has to say something. Let me see." Amy plucked the fortune right out of Judy's hand.

"Don't worry!" said Amy. "It's not a real fortune! It's written on a sticky note. In kid handwriting."

"Something tells me it just might come true anyway," said Judy.

By the next Tuesday, Classes 3T and 3V had traveled the world for seven days. The next day was the last day. The next day was Day Eight. There was only one problem. Rocky and Frank were still M-A-D mad. Madder than a spider bite. Madder than a tarantula dancing the tarantella.

She, Judy Moody, was in a mood. She had a bad case of the DIY Blues. The Do-It-Yourself Blues. Judy always heard Mom and Dad saying, "If you want to get something done, do it yourself." Maybe she *could* do the dance without Rocky and Frank. Jessica Finch, too. When Rocky and Frank saw how hard she worked on their Around-the-World project, she would save them from flunking and they wouldn't be mad anymore.

So she, Judy Moody, official card-carrying member of the My-Name-Is-a-Poem Club, would make sure Classes 3T and 3V went around the world in eight days. She, Judy Moody, would DIH. Do. It. Herself.

Judy stayed up past bedtime reading about Italy and gluing pizza tables together and making up a game for everyone to play. She even made Stink practice the tarantella with her, but he just kept stomping on her feet.

When she woke up the next morning, she dressed in a red skirt and a green-and-white striped shirt. She even drew Italian flags on her white tights and wore her red shoes from the time she was Dorothy for Halloween.

"Who are you?" asked Stink. "One of Santa's elves?"

"Elf schmelf," said Judy. "Don't you know what's red, white, and green all over?"

"Markers that got on Mom's new white carpet?" asked Stink.

"I hope you're kidding," said Mom. "Hmm, let's see. Red, white, and green. How about that strange spaghetti Dad makes?"

"I thought you liked my tri-color pasta," said Dad. "You said it was creative!"

"It's creative all right," said Mom, making a funny face.

"Well, I hope we're not having that tonight," said Judy. "Because I borrowed lots of pasta for my Pasta Shapes Game."

"Okay, I'll bite," said Dad. "What's red, white, and green all over? A Christmas zebra?"

"No-o!" said Judy. "It has nothing to do with Christmas."

"I know!" said Stink. "How about the flag of Bulgaria, Hungary, Mexico, or Madagascar?"

"Mad-at-what-car? Hello! How about It-a-ly, Stink? The flag of Italy is red, white, and green."

"I can't help it. I didn't read the *I* volume of the encyclopedia yet," said Stink. "Besides, you don't look like a flag. And I should know. I was a human flag once. . . ."

"Wow, this must be quite a project," said Dad.

"It is," said Judy. "It took Nellie Bly seventy-two days to go around the world, and she beat the record. Try going around the whole world in just eight days!"

"So, are you and your friends all patched up now?" asked Mom.

"It's still a little rocky," said Judy. "But after today—"

"A little *Rocky*? Get it?" asked Stink.

"Ha, ha," said Judy. "Stink, can I borrow

your tarantula skeleton to take to school? And your tambourine?"

"I don't know," said Stink. "I'll think about it."

"Stink, don't be a *bratellino*. Not today. Please."

"Do they have a lot of tarantulas and tambourines in Italy or something?" asked Stink.

"Or something," said Judy.

"No, I mean it," said Stink.

"Stink, for a kid who reads the encyclopedia, you sure don't know a lot of stuff."

"I haven't read the *T* volume yet either!" said Stink.

"Well, you better get cracking!" said

Judy. "Didn't you know? In the country of Italy, tarantulas play the tambourine while eating tortellini!"

Red-White-and-Green Machine

When Judy got to school that morning, she bumped into Amy Namey in the hall.

"I can't wait to hear about Italy!" said Amy. "We get to come over to your class again. I can't wait to see your group dance that spider dance!"

"*I'm* my group," said Judy. She stepped inside Class 3T and set the Leaning Tower of Pizza Tables on the shelf by the window.

She covered it with an upside-down box so nobody would see it yet.

"Rocky, did you bring the record? And the record player?" asked Judy.

"Frank," said Rocky, "tell Judy I brought the record player."

"Yipes stripes! You're still not talking to me?" asked Judy.

Rocky zipped his lips.

"Lipper Zipper," said Judy, cracking herself up.

"Huh?" asked Frank.

"Never mind," said Judy. "You had to be there. And I was. With Amy Namey. Not you guys!"

As soon as the bell rang, it was time for Judy's group to tell about Italy. Judy and Jessica stood up in front of Class 3T and Class 3V.

"Judy," asked Mr. Todd, "what about the rest of your group?"

"C'mon, you guys," Judy whispered.

Rocky and Frank came and stood up front. "Um, Rocky's having trouble with his voice or something," said Judy. "So I'll be talking for my group. Frank will hold up the flag of Italy." Judy handed the flag to Frank.

"*Ciao,* everybody," said Judy. "First, Jessica Finch will pass out a Pizza Spelling Test."

"Test!?" everybody complained.

"It's just for fun," said Jessica. "And you can do it whenever you want. It's not like it's H-O-M-E-W-O-R-K or anything."

"Now," said Judy Moody, "first I'll tell you a little about Italy. Then we'll play a game, and I'll show you a dance. So, Italy sure has some funny-sounding cities. Like Baloney, Italy. And Pizza, Italy."

"It's Ba-LONE-ya," said Mr. Todd. "And PEE-za, Italy."

"*Bravo!*" said Judy. "In the town of Pizza, there's this tower, but it's crooked. So it's called the Leaning Tower of Pizza."

"And guess what?" said Jessica Finch. "If you mess up the letters in THE LEAN-ING TOWER OF PISA, you get WHAT A

FOREIGN STONE PILE. It's called an anagram."

"Anyway," said Judy, "I made a leaning tower to show you what it looks like."

"That was our idea!" said Rocky.

"Rocky, I see you found your voice," said Mr. Todd.

"This was Rocky and Frank's idea," said Judy. *"Voilà!"*

"Voilà is French," said Jessica Finch. "We learned that last week."

"May I present," said Judy, "the Leaning Tower of Pizza Tables." She yanked off the box.

Something was not right! The Leaning Tower of Pizza Tables wasn't leaning at all.

It was *melted*. What used to be a leaning stack of glued-together pizza tables was now just a great big globby blob of melty plastic.

"Ahhh!" Everybody pointed and cracked up.

"I'm melting!" said Rocky in a Wicked-Witch-of-the-West voice.

"Oh, no!" said Judy. "My Leaning Tower of Pizza Tables. I set it on the shelf . . . over the radiator!"

"The heat melted them," said Rocky.

"We'll just have to call it the Melted Tower of Pizza," said Frank.

"Don't feel bad," said Amy Namey. "That's like what happened to my papier-mâché globe. Globe explode! Remember?"

"Okay, folks, the show must go on!" said Mr. Todd.

Judy took out the supplies for the Pasta Shapes Game.

"Everybody gets their own game board and a little bag with pasta in it," said Judy, holding up a bag and rattling it. "You match the different kinds of pasta in the bag with the shapes on your board."

"Great idea," said Mr. Todd.

"That sounds like lots of fun," said Ms. Valentine.

"Then write the name of the noodle under it. If you don't know the name, you can look up at my chart." Judy held up a piece of cardboard that had pasta shapes glued onto it. Above each kind of pasta was its name.

PASTAS FROM ITALY

CAPPellini	Penne	elbow macaroni
FARfalle	Rotini	fettuccine
spaghetti	fusilli	linguine
Vermicelli	Pastina	Ziti
ravioli	tortellini	pappardelle

Everybody cracked up. "Ha, ha!" Bradley pointed.

"You're missing some," said a kid from the other class.

"Where's the elbow macaroni?" somebody asked.

"And the vermicelli? And the cappellini?" asked Jessica.

Judy stared at her cardboard. How could she have missed any? She had even stayed up late making sure she had every single last one glued into place.

She marched over to Rocky and Frank. "Which one of you stole them? Give it." She held out her hand.

"I didn't do anything! Honest!" said Rocky.

Frank was chewing away on something. And the something was not gum. The something was pasta shapes from her game.

"You ate them!?" cried Judy.

"I got hungry just standing here being a flag," mumbled Frank.

"Eeuw! Use your noodle, Frank," she said, pointing to her head. "Those noodles were not even cooked!"

"So?" said Frank. "They still taste good."

"Yuck!" said Judy. "They had GLUE on them. I'm going to tell the whole world that you, Frank Pearl, ate glue."

"So? Everybody thinks I eat paste anyway."

"ROAR-a-lini!" said Judy.

The Leaning Tower of Pizza Tables had melted. The Pasta Shapes Game had gotten eaten. Getting around the world in eight days was definitely not easy.

But nothing could wreck the tarantella. Nothing. It had to be perfect. If only she hadn't forgotten about the practice that day. Now she, Judy Moody, would dance the tarantella alone. Just like her fortune had said.

Rocky would play the record. Frank would shake the tambourine. And Jessica Finch would clap along.

She could not mess this up, or half the third grade would be mad that they did not make it around the world in eight days.

While everyone finished the Pasta Shapes Game, Mr. Todd pushed desks and stuff over to the corner so Judy would have plenty of room.

"Okey-dokey," said Judy. "This morning I am going to dance the tarantella."

"The tarantula?" somebody asked.

"No, not the tarantula," said Frank.

"Well, actually, you're never going to believe it, but I looked it up. Who knew? *Tarantella* means 'tarantula.' For real and absolute positive. My dad told me the dance started a long time ago, before he was even born, around the Middle Ages." Mr. Todd and Ms. Valentine cracked up.

Judy held up the tarantula skin in a bag. Everybody squirmed. "EEUW!"

"Don't worry, it's not a real spider. Just the skin or the skeleton of a tarantula. Anyway, this dance is called the Spider Dance. Some people say it started because if you got bitten by a tarantula, then you'd act as crazy as a loon and dance to get all the spider-bite stuff out of your system. A doctor even wrote about it and said this dance was a cure for spider bites."

"Interesting," Mr. Todd said, raising his eyebrows.

"A spider has eight legs, so usually you need four people," said Judy, glancing over at Rocky, Frank, and Jessica.

"Judy," said Mr. Todd, "why don't you show us? Then we'll call on some others to come up and try it with you."

"*Fantastico!*" said Judy. Rocky started the record. Judy faced the third graders. She stretched her hands in the air. Frank started to shake the tambourine. Jessica Finch clapped. Judy took a deep breath. "Nice and easy," she told herself.

Da da da, duh da da da,

Da da da-da-da-da-duh

Step-hop, slide. Step-hop, slide. Change step. Hop. Skip. Slap knee. Repeat. Buzz turn. Spin in place.

"One, two, three, and four," Judy counted to herself. She tried to remember all the steps she practiced. She tried to remember to reverse direction when the music changed. She tried to keep up with the music as it got faster.

Stephopslide. Stephopslide. Change!
Step! Hop! Skip! Slapknee! Repeat!

Da da da, duh da da da,
Da da da-da-da-da-duh

Something was not right! The music was too fast!

Judy made her feet go faster and faster until her head was dizzy and her hair was in her mouth.

"Too—*puff puff*—fast!" she panted. "Slow—*puff puff*—down!" *Huff puff puff.*

But nobody seemed to hear. The music kept going faster and faster. Frank shook the tambourine faster than an earthquake. Judy whirled and twirled, a dizzy dancing dervish. Her feet were moving so fast, she felt like a spider with eight legs.

The class was clapping and shouting and laughing and pointing. Mr. Todd blinked the lights. Judy spun like a top out of control—a dizzy, dancing, red-white-and-green machine!

Suddenly, she banged into a desk, tripped over her own foot, and fell in a red, white, and green heap on the floor.

"Oops. Was it too fast?" Rocky asked innocently.

"*Stupido!*" Judy mumbled.

She, Judy Moody, knew that Rocky and Frank had revved up the tarantella music on purpose.

It was just plain red, white, and mean.

Eatsa Pizza

The tarantella had turned out to be a big fat flop. Nobody with *two* legs could dance as fast as a spider with *eight* legs. Now the third graders would not make it around the world in eight days. And everybody would blame her, even though she had danced her legs off!

She, Judy Moody, had flunked.

It was all Rocky and Frank's fault. Rocky No-Talky and Frank the Prank. The My-Name-Is-NOT-a-Poem Club.

After Class 3V left the room, Mr. Todd had a private talk with Judy, Rocky, Frank, and Jessica. He talked to them about what it means to work together as a group. He wanted them to work out their differences, to give each other a second chance. He wanted them to be friends again. But most of all, *he* wanted to give *them* a second chance.

"Do I have to have a second chance?" asked Jessica. "Because I think I tried to be a T-E-A-M P-L-A-Y-E-R."

"You know," said Mr. Todd, "in Italy there's a saying. 'You have to break a few eggs to make an omelet.'"

"For real?" said Judy.

"Absolutely," said Mr. Todd. "Things

often go wrong before they go right. It happens all the time."

"I've heard of 'break a leg' but never 'break an egg,'" said Jessica.

"Boys, how about if I give you until tomorrow morning to do your part for our Around-the-World unit?" Mr. Todd said.

"You mean we could still think up our own Italy project, and bring it in tomorrow morning?" asked Rocky.

"And then we'd still get to go around the world, even though it took eight and a half days?" asked Frank.

"I don't see why not," said Mr. Todd. "Even Nellie Bly had a lot of things go wrong on her trip around the world."

"Yeah, like there was a bad storm and she almost didn't make it back to America on time," said Jessica.

"And McGinty, her monkey, got scared and jumped on a lady's back!" said Judy. "Everybody said he was bad luck and wanted Nellie to throw him overboard!"

"That's right," said Mr. Todd. "So, what do you say? Sound like a plan?"

"It's a plan," said Rocky and Frank.

Rocky turned to Judy. "We're sorry you did all the work and for messing up your dance," said Rocky. "You were REALLY fast! So fast it looked like you had eight legs!"

"And we're sorry for eating your Pasta Shapes Game and for getting mad," said Frank. "We really messed up."

"I messed up, too," said Judy. "I'm the one who missed our practice. All I could think about was the My-Name-Is-a-Poem Club, and I guess I forgot my old friends." She held out a hand. Rocky and Frank piled their hands on top of hers.

"Don't forget me!" said Jessica, adding her hand to the top of the pile.

☙ ☙ ☙

Magnifico! Fantastico! Judy could not wait to tell Amy Namey that Classes 3T and 3V were going to go around the world in eight (and a half) days after all!

Rocky and Frank had to think up a project. Fast. And Judy and Jessica did not even have to help. Mr. Todd said the boys needed to figure it out all by themselves.

"So what are you going to do?" Judy asked them.

"It's a surprise," said Frank.

"It's a really big scoop," said Rocky.

"Well, it better not be the Leaning Tower

of Pizza Tables again, because half my collection melted."

"It'll be better," said Frank.

"It'll be big," said Rocky.

"It'll be red, white, and green!" said Rocky and Frank, cracking themselves up.

"Is it . . . the Grinch . . . on a fire engine?" Jessica guessed.

"You'll see," said Rocky.

"You'll see," said Frank.

"Break an egg!" said Judy.

The next morning, Rocky was not on the bus. And Judy was dying to show him the letter and the photo she'd gotten from Nathaniel Daniel in California.

When Judy got to school, she ran over to Amy's class.

"Look what I got!" she told Amy Namey.

"It's Bubblegum Alley!" said Amy.

"Look closer," Judy said.

Amy peered at the photo and found the initials *JM* made out of chewed-up gum.

"*JM* for *Judy Moody*! I'm on the Wall of Gum!" said Judy. "In the Bubblegum Hall of Fame."

"Double check!" said Amy.

"Hey, have you seen Rocky? Or Frank?" Judy asked Jessica Finch when she got to class.

"Didn't you hear? The two of them got here super early and they've been down in the cafeteria all morning. I can't wait to find out what they're up to." The whole class was buzzing about the big scoop. Rocky and Frank even got to miss Spelling.

Finally, Rocky and Frank came back upstairs. They told Mr. Todd and Ms. Valentine to bring everybody down to the cafeteria in five minutes.

"What *IS* it?" asked Judy, rushing up to Rocky and Frank.

"We're not telling!" they said.

Class 3T and Class 3V walked single file down the hall and down the stairs to the cafeteria. They could smell it before they saw it. Everybody had a seat at one of the lunch tables.

The project was so big, it would not fit through the door, so the lunch ladies had to help them slide it through the wide window from the kitchen. In came a lunch lady, then Rocky, then Frank, then another lunch lady. They were holding their hands over their heads and carrying the biggest, roundest circle of cardboard Judy had ever seen.

"YUM!" said Jessica Finch.

"Smells good!" said Judy.

"What is it?" everybody asked.

It took six pushed-together tables just to hold it. They set the cardboard down. On it was the biggest, bubbliest, yummiest, cheesiest pizza in the world.

"What's red, white, and green all over?" asked Frank.

"The World's Biggest Pizza!" Rocky announced. "Red sauce and white cheese with green-pepper topping!"

"No way!" everybody said.

"Yah-huh," said Rocky. "At least it's Virginia Dare School's Biggest-Ever Pizza. It's six feet wide, and we used thirty pounds of dough and thirty-six pounds of cheese."

"That pizza weighs more than me!" shouted Judy.

"Actually," said Frank, "the real World's Biggest Pizza is about the size of a parking lot."

"But this *is* the World's Biggest Pizza *Map!*" said Rocky.

"What? Huh?"

Everybody gathered around the pizza and took a closer look. It was big and round as a world, and the cheese was piled in seven funny shapes. One for each continent. Like a map! Green peppers made a trail from North America to the tip of Asia.

"I get it! It's a map!"

"It's the world!"

"I see North America!"

"I see Italy! It's the shape of a boot," said Judy.

"Look!" said Amy Namey. "The pizza map follows Nellie Bly's trip around the world."

"Right—it's all the places we went around the world in eight and a half days," said Judy.

Amy Namey took out her clipboard. "I'm going to be first to get the big scoop," she told Judy. "I'll write this up for my newspaper! WORLD'S BIGGEST PIZZA MAP AT VIRGINIA DARE SCHOOL."

"Don't forget CLASS 3T AND 3V GO AROUND THE WORLD IN EIGHT AND A HALF DAYS!" said Judy.

"Eight and a half days, two hours, thirteen minutes, and twenty-seven seconds," said Amy, looking at both her watches.

"Check!" said Rocky and Frank, sounding like Amy Namey.

"*Fantastico!*" said Judy.

"Dig in!" said a lunch lady. "There's more than enough for everybody."

"There's more than enough to have pizza for lunch every day for a week!" said Rocky.

"Pizza for lunch every day? Told you that could happen," said Amy Namey.

Magnifico!

Judy and Rocky and Frank and Amy each picked up a slice. A string of ooey-gooey cheese stretched from Rocky's to Frank's to Judy's to Amy's slice of pizza.

"Hey! We're all connected!" said Judy.

"The Eatsa Pizza Club!" said Frank.

"Double cool," said Rocky.

"Triple yum," said Frank.

"Quadruple check!" said Amy Namey.

And the four friends laughed themselves red, white, and green all over. Then they sat down and ate the biggest, cheesiest, most *delizioso* pizza in the world.

For sure and absolute *positivo*!

Megan McDonald —————— is the award-winning author of the Judy Moody series. She says that most of Judy's stories "come from anecdotes about growing up with my four sisters." She confesses, "I *am* Judy Moody. Same-same! In my family of sisters, we're famous for exaggeration. Judy Moody is me . . . exaggerated." Megan McDonald lives with her husband in northern California.

Peter H. Reynolds —————— says he felt an immediate connection to Judy Moody because, "having a daughter, I have witnessed firsthand the adventures of a very independent-minded girl." Peter H. Reynolds lives in Massachusetts, just down the street from his twin brother.

Look out, Judy Moody!

Stink

is starring in his very own series!

Here's a sneak peek at Stink's first adventure!

The bell rang, and Mrs. Dempster passed out spelling words. Three of the new words were *shrink, shrank, shrunk.* At lunch, the dessert was strawberry *short*cake. And in Reading, Mrs. Dempster read everybody a book called *The Shrinking of Treehorn.*

The book was all about a boy who plays games and reads cereal boxes and gets shorter and shorter. He keeps shrinking and shrinking. Then, just when he becomes a normal size again, he turns green!

"Any comments?" Mrs. Dempster asked when the story was over.

Stink raised his hand. "Is that a true story?"

Mrs. D. laughed. "I'm afraid not," she said. "It's fantasy."

"Fantasy's my favorite!" said Sophie of the Elves. "Especially hobbits and elves."

"Are you sure it's fantasy?" asked Stink.

"Because that kid is a lot like me. Because I'm . . . I'm . . ." Stink could not make himself say *shrinking.*

"Because you both turned another color?" asked Webster.

"Um, because I like to read everything on the cereal box, too," said Stink.

"Okay," said Mrs. Dempster. "Let's see. Who's going to carry the milk from the cafeteria today?" Stink was barely paying attention. He never got asked to carry the milk.

"How about Mr. James Moody?" asked Mrs. Dempster.

"Me?" asked Stink. He sat up taller. "I get to carry the milk?"

Stink walked down the second-grade hallway. It looked longer than usual. And wider. He took the stairs down to the cafeteria. Were there always so many stairs? His legs felt shorter. Like they shrink, shrank, shrunk.

Be sure to check out
Stink's adventures!

Experience
all of
Judy Moody's
moods!

Judy Moody Was in a mood. Not a good mood. A bad mood.

Megan McDonald   illustrated by Peter H. Reynolds

Judy Moody Gets Famous!

Megan McDonald   illustrated by Peter H. Reynolds

Judy Moody Saves the World!

Megan McDonald   illustrated by Peter H. Reynolds

Judy Moody Predicts the Future

Megan McDonald   illustrated by Peter H. Reynolds

Judy Moody, M.D. The Doctor Is In!

Megan McDonald   illustrated by Peter H. Reynolds

Judy Moody Declares Independence

Megan McDonald   illustrated by Peter H. Reynolds

THE JUDY MOODY MOOD JOURNAL

Megan McDonald   illustrated by Peter H. Reynolds

Judy Moody's

INCLUDES 24 STICKERS INSIDE!

Double-Rare Way-Not-Boring Book of Fun Stuff to Do

Megan McDonald   illustrated by Peter H. Reynolds

DOUBLE RARE!
Judy Moody has her own website!

Come visit **www.judymoody.com**
for the latest in all things Judy Moody, including:

- ❀ All you need to know about the best-ever Judy Moody Fan Club

- ❀ Answers to all your V.I.Q.s (very important questions) about Judy

- ❀ Way-not-boring stuff about Megan McDonald and Peter H. Reynolds

- ❀ Double-cool activities that will be sure to put you in a mood—and not a bad mood, a good mood!

- ❀ Totally awesome T.P. Club info!